DECEPTION PASS

Latitude 48°24'25" N
Longitude 122°38'46" W

DECEPTION PASS

SUE STANDING

Alice James Books   Cambridge, Massachusetts

Cover art and design by Mark Wethli
Book design & typesetting by Ed Hogan/Type for U
Pasteup by Lea Cyr/Type for U

The publication of this book was made possible with support
from the Massachusetts Council on the Arts and Humanities,
a state agency whose funds are recommended by the Governor
and appropriated by the State Legislature.

Library of Congress Catalogue Card Number 84-70354
ISBN 0-914086-50-2 (hardbound)
ISBN 0-914086-51-0 (paperback)

Alice James Books are published by
the Alice James Poetry Cooperative, Inc.

Alice James Books
138 Mount Auburn Street
Cambridge, Massachusetts 02138

ACKNOWLEDGEMENTS

The poems in this book first appeared in the following publications:

THE AGNI REVIEW: The Very Rich Hours
THE AMERICAN POETRY REVIEW: Hopper's Women
THE AMERICAN SCHOLAR: Dead Neck
BLACK/& WHITE LINES: Fortune's Fortune, Mozartiana
BLUE UNICORN: Family
BOSTONIA: Lullaby
CONFRONTATION: What Can Be Changed
HARVARD ADVOCATE: Steptoe Butte
HARVARD MAGAZINE: Birches
MISSISSIPPI VALLEY REVIEW: Watermark
MT. SAN ANGELO SERIES, #1: Swimming Lessons for the Dead,
    Letter to St. Jerome
THE OHIO REVIEW: Returning the Evidence
PALE FIRE REVIEW: The Coming of the Ice Age, Elegy for
    Ralph Eugene Meatyard
PLOUGHSHARES: Convict's Mirror, Mostly Departures
POET LORE: The Schumann Duet, Heartprint, Getting Off
    the Train, Vocabulary
THE RADCLIFFE QUARTERLY: A Woman Disappears Inside
    Her Own Life
SALMAGUNDI: A Blind Woman in the Wood
SEATTLE REVIEW: Witness
WIND: June 21

"Cellar Door," "Hopper's Women," and "Aubade: Portrait with Shadows" also appeared in a chapbook, *Amphibious Weather*, published by Zephyr Press.

"Dead Neck" was included in the 1981 *Anthology of Magazine Verse and Yearbook of American Poetry.* "Vocabulary" will appear in the 1984 *Anthology of Magazine Verse and Yearbook of American Poetry.*

I wish to thank the Bunting Institute of Radcliffe College, The MacDowell Colony, The Millay Colony for the Arts, Virginia Center for the Creative Arts, and Yaddo for their generous support. Special thanks to Miriam Sagan, Kendra Kopelke, Henry Fox, my writing group, and the poets of AJB for their help in preparing this manuscript.

CONTENTS

in memory of my mother,
Beverly Farnes Standing
1926-1975

I

THE VERY RICH HOURS

1. Matins

Today is a holiday in the country of goodbye.
I wake to birds crashing into windows
and to heat. There's a horseshoe crab ballet
in the bay and wasp music on the radio.
No one is on the horizon, no one is praying
to Our Lady of Perpetual Loneliness.
In the inner dark, I still count the ribs
of sleep, a halo of moths around my head.
I dream I love the simple
and enter the museum of my past
where objects are losing their luminescence,
their specific properties of association,
and those beautiful marbles, the planets,
generate cyclones that will last a million years.

2. Lauds

Praise primary colors, ascensions, assumptions,
and questions of attribution. Praise tablets,
erasures, names, and the luxury of personality.
Which world is this? The one with precise
collisions of molecules or the one with skies
trimmed in gold stars? How do I get from
atoms of blue paint in the book of hours
to your irradiated face? From the blue motes
on the painter's wrist to the blue veins beneath?
From the gravid light of late summer
to the blank white facades of funeral homes?
Praise drumlins, druids, and diatoms.
Praise daylight savings and another hour
to bloom and ache under the blue dome.

3. Mass

I am reading about celestial navigation
for the simpleminded, about dark nebulae
born out of clouds of obscuring dust—
I squint into the sky from the hammock,
but there are hours of daylight left—
and star temperature mapped with respect
to luminosity, not mass but light.
I try to imagine the speed at which
all bodies in the universe are dashing
away from each other. But I keep thinking
of that boat with its cargo of ashes
scattered each week along the coastline,
of mourning pictures with weeping willows
embroidered in black thread, tears, and hair.

4. *Sext*

Unnatural habitats: the rain, for instance,
falling in the delicate porch of your ear;
or a choice of skies—a modern one by Kline,
bold strokes, or Tiepolo's, too pink and sweet;
or a glacial cirque shaped like the hollow
at the base of your throat; or the cupid
in the boxwood labyrinth, presiding
over meandering lovers with a leer,
one stone wing fallen to the ground
by the limestone plinth. I pick up the broken
wing, so heavy after yesterday's swallowtail,
dead wings still brushed with pollen dust.
I look for you inside a disc of leaves
and the cut wood, cut heart of a beech.

5. *None*

A wedge, natural architect of distance
lets the liquid film of light ring glasses
empty of air, keeps love from spilling like
xenon out of the lamps and into the artichokes
arranged like topiary trees on the table.
Now, the mirror peels off layers of my face,
down to the quicksilver and flakes of mica,
each time I eat with my father's knives, or
raise my mother's crystal to my lips.
But all I ever wanted was to be
located on the plumb line of history,
only to reach the circle of gold and coffee
on the equator, looking for the lost infinitives,
my lost: to be, to build, to bloom.

6. *Vespers*

I remember an evening like this one,
but in the city, where still as husband
and wife on an Etruscan sarcophagus,
we tried to evade the heat,
heavy air our blanket of stone,
shadows like palm fronds falling
through the blinds. We knew the city
by echolocation, could feel the traffic
bob and weave below, as your mouth
told a story of lovers tangled
like seaweed at the bottom of a pool.
Words settled between us, calm dust
of mind. For once, our bodies
were not singing, "refrain, refrain."

7. *Compline*

The full moon rises over the pitched roof
of the barn, between cupola and silo.
Someone is playing guitar under the hickory,
folk songs, half-remembered verses,
partial harmonies, off-notes sweetened
by the dusky air. Quick shadow,
a dragonfly lands on my knee.
I repeat the names of wildflowers over and over,
and still they will not stay on my tongue.
They disappear as quickly as drops of water
on your cast iron stove, or the hummingbird
in the hollyhocks. You turn to me and say:
"Name the parts of the heart."
I thought the heart was one piece.

II

A BLIND WOMAN IN THE WOOD

(after an etching by Paula Modersohn-Becker)

The way mushrooms settle
in a cup of light,
the way the dust

of bean vines culled
summer after summer
gathers in her breath—

she knows the untouched
circle of pine needles
beneath the tree.

Her hands are indian pipes,
the twigs of leafless trees,
white against the black

of her curved shoulders
sloping to the ground.
Tendrils of her shawl take root.

She knows the smell of moss
and violets, unravels the dark,
a stick poked in a wasps' nest.

She will wander deeper,
but who would lead her back
once they saw the constellation—

lattice, fanlight, oriel—
a grid of light
grazing her face.

HOPPER'S WOMEN

for Libby Hodges

1. House by the Railroad

She minds the lilacs.
What can be saved, she saves:
dried flowers, tarnished costume jewelry,
half-used boxes of face powder.
She imagines a man will call to her from the train:
"The fruits of summer are here!"
Sun pierces the house like the whistle
of the train. Inside she waits,
knitting the heavy light of afternoon.
A few pieces of Sandwich glass
glow in the windows.
The aspidistra, which never grows,
throws spiky shadows at her feet.

2. East Side Interior

She minds the cool
moonshine in the room.
In the frame of the window,
her soft profile, dark mass of hair,
she bends low, sewing.
Her African violets bloom all winter.
She thinks bones, she thinks rivers,
she thinks bread and yeast,
the way the white curtain
billows over the bed.
She will stay at the window through dusk
like a ghost at the sewing machine,
opaque and beautiful and lost.

3. Nighthawks

She minds her cheap gardenia perfume,
her tight red dress.
The way this reflection goes,
she sees only her angular arms
and the drugstore counter;
neon blots out the rest, except for fragments
of her dress mirrored on the coffee urn.
The men can't figure why she comes here,
night after night.
They haven't seen her room and won't.
She wonders why she can't leave
the harsh light of this town, wonders
if every town contains only two stories.

THE SCHUMANN DUET

"Between the lines of this letter,
invisible writing one day will appear."
Robert, I start this with your words,
the way my father when I was five,
wrote for me in my new book:
"Today my father divorced my mother."
He wanted me to be a concert pianist,
no hausfrau. This morning,
one of your "papillons" hovered
between me and the keys.
I could not play the simplest tune.
You always ask for flowers, never for news of me.

The critics praise my technique, "Clara,
your wrists are delicate, but strong,"
and dismiss my concerto, "the work of a lady."
My composing all behindhand,
you said, "Children are blessings."
Now our eldest daughter writes:
"I saw my father for the last time
the day he went out to take his life"—
walking on tiptoe to the Rhine
wearing only slippers and a dressing gown.
Will the asylum ever give you up?
I keep the children working on their scales.

From Endenich, Johannes writes he finds you
cutting up atlases, planning a trip
city to city, by strict alphabet.
You tell him, "I still get pleasure
from the palindrome-riddle Roma-Amor."
Your "nine-fingered" self which used
to joke and pluck the notes from air
now pulls feathers from the counterpane.
Something vibrates four-hundred-forty times
each second, within your ears—
lately, I think I hear it, too—
a perfect A, perfect.

MOZARTIANA

The drawing room stiffness dissolves
around the coffin of the grand piano,

but all the mouths are still closed
with sealing wax or honey.

I long for the planet of pure music,
the songs divested of their skins,

where a touch of the keys unlocks the nerves,
where sounds create the world that's seen—

the way the compound eye records a knife
composed of leaves of light.

FORTUNE'S FORTUNE

An angular woman with a belt
of stars, you hum in the morning.

The cave of the winds is nothing
next to the motion of your chemise.

Salmon climb the ladder
of veins above your wrist.

Light touches your shoulders,
polished and naked epaulettes.

I watch your face watching
your palm tell me everything.

TWO KWAKIUTL MASKS

1. Dzoonokwa
   the cannibal woman

she comes with her streams of hair
the fish climb into her belly
her mouth is a wind a warning
there is no bottom to her basket

a giant woman with no mate
she places children in her womb
that other women have birthed
her blood grows stronger

she sends one mad eye inward
opens her wide mouth
and shakes the forest with her cries
her footprints hold echoes
big as whaling canoes

2. Bukwus
    the wild man of the woods

sends rain
brings nightmares

spirit of those
almost drowned

he scatters ash
circles the fire

enters the rim
of an eye

part bird
eats bone

sings a song
only women can hear.

CONVICT'S MIRROR

I bang my spoon on the table,
my iron tongue.

To calm myself I try to remember
the weight of a cubic foot of water,

count the layers of whitewash
scaling the walls.

Outside is a mild apricot
evening, evangelist air.

Everything is far away,
there are no stairs.

Send me a package
of unbarred air,

slip a parcel of dust
over the transom.

I'm tired of a face
fissured in metal,

a voice neutral
as a polltaker's.

I'm tired of grieving
in a house full of mutes,

we can't cry out loud.
I try to picture myself:

I'm in a purple light,
mercury locking my eyelids,

my limbs arranged
on the perfect sheet.

ELEGY FOR RALPH EUGENE MEATYARD

(1925-1972)

South of here
your ashes are scattered
under the dogwood.
Optician, photographer:
how did you grind the lenses
for your own strange visions?

I wonder if your giant
eyeglasses still hang
in Lexington, Kentucky.
Are Lucybelle Crater and her friend,
Lucybelle Crater, still swinging
on the front porch?

The transparent masks may drift
in the branches of trees
through all seasons.
Perhaps you wished for the velvet
curtains, the shadowboxes,
the photographers' hoods.

The air in your photographs
is thick with lace and leaves.
The world whirls around each figure:
one man steps into a square of sunlight—
blurred sex, face masked,
one leg dematerialized as it moves.

Your friend with the hook for a hand
stands next to a dressmaker's dummy,
exchanging the tension of animation
across a blank mirror.
And your camera has found the children
lost in the fields.

One face scarred with light
is next to a cracked globe of the world,
a skeleton drawing, and blisters of pigment.
Something will last, even when the page
curls at the edge, and only the shadows
of eyes remain at the center.

III

Now I knew I lost her -
Not that she was gone -
But Remoteness travelled -
On her Face and Tongue.

Alien, though adjoining
As a Foreign Race -
Traversed she though pausing
Latitudeless Place.

—Emily Dickinson

JUNE 21

The Osterville cemetery is full
of the Lovells and their dogs.
Lovell—must be short for
"love well." Wrinkled stones
say the earth has loved
their bones a long time.

As I walk I think of the package
from my father,
glass broken in the mail—
a photograph of my mother
smiling, wearing a blue-green dress.
3000 miles away, a bronze slab
etched with dogwood marks her grave.
She would have been fifty.

Bobwhite, otherwise
all is quiet.

I want my father pitching horseshoes
in the backyard, my mother plucking
a chicken in the kitchen, us kids
playing "no bears are out tonight
daddy shot them all last night."
I want to be home where the peace
roses must have opened and bloomed
as always on her birthday.

CELLAR DOOR

A room to go to—
not lapidary windows,
but jars which hold the light of fruit,
the taste of summer, and my mother's labor.
In winter, I open the knotty pine door,
hide from my sister and brothers,
read *Little Women* and *The Secret Garden*.

My mother stands at the sink all summer
as the fruits succeed each other—
strawberries, cherries, peaches, apricots, apples.
The huge blue enamelled cauldron
steams on the stove.
She wipes the sweat from her forehead
with a dishcloth.

At the center of all this ripeness,
her hands of fruit and sun.
Spearmint strained through cheesecloth.
Scalded mason jars lined up on the embroidered tablecloth.
Stacks of shiny metal lids and sealing rings
(used for gypsy bracelets at Halloween).
I sneak sweet froth skimmed from the top of jams.

Her hands stained and nicked
from all the peeling, cutting, blanching—
beautiful how they touched things,
how quickly she could thread a needle.
I'm not supposed to love her for this—
smoothing our hair, sewing our clothes,
or on her knees waxing the floor.

I see the blur of her smile,
her smile that hid so much.
I saw her cry only a few times,
when she could not hold us after her operations,
and when she told me once she was afraid,
and I could not look at her
for fear of her fear.

I remember the sound of the jars sealing at night
as if something were alive in each,
kicking to get out: first one jar, then another,
a chorus of pops and smacks like frogs on a pond.
Then the careful carrying down to cellar,
and the winter choosing of fruit for breakfast.
When I chose, I chose by color not by taste.

I open the door so slowly,
feel the knots in the wood.
She told me here one day that I should cultivate desire.
I was surprised.
I had never connected my mother with desire,
and could not ask her if she meant a strong will,
an earthly passion, or a clear heart.

I come to this room
where there is no longer fruit on the shelves,
only cases of tin-canned goods,
gallons drums of wheat and emergency water,
a strong smell of must.
I wish I could find just one jar overlooked,
one jar of clearest mint.

A flickering leaf-veined pattern
falls on the floor
like a hand in front of a candle flame,
her hand on my forehead,
as if the last rooms of memory
hold only light.

WATERMARK

for my mother

She is carrying the first flowers
I remember, the irises
which grew by the house.
She is carrying flowers,
an armload, and singing.
Her face is free of pain,
the flowers light her face.
She is carrying herself
toward the threshold.
She tries to throw the flowers
across the river to me,
but they float downstream.

*

My sister and I, one summer,
took lifesaving. We had to practice
mouth-to-mouth on each other.
We imagined our mouths

were the mouths of fishes,
the hooks caught in our cheeks.
We gathered silver grunion
in nets under the full moon.

Though we once invented a language
secret from our parents and brothers,
speech was never our territory.
And so we have come here together

to Deception Pass—our voices lost
as Vancouver in the rush of water
deep in the gorge—looking for clues
to our mother's unwritten life:

the trips to Snoqualmie Falls,
ferry rides in Puget Sound,
and, most of all, the half-built
houses on Sunday afternoons.

Something in her hands
needed new wood, the smooth
compline of a plane,
chains of shavings hemming her.

*

I used to wonder if my hands
would become like my mother's:
raised veins, liver spots,
ridged and striated fingernails.
Like hers, my hands are always cold.

Once, in a fever, I thought I saw
my mother standing in the doorway,
a cool cloth in her hands.
She laid the cloth on my forehead
and stroked my hair.

Soothed, I went to sleep,
and woke in a strange room,
still feeling her touch.
Now I spend dreams threading a needle,
sewing shrouds from the cypresses.

*

Rain flattens the river,
the wind a bridge of white
stones along the way.

A dress primed with roses
husks her body, she sleeps
in a pocket of green.

Now her life inhabits
my life, her shadow
stitches itself to mine.

We share a small light—clouds
furrowed instead of fields,
white stones, a long way home.

FAMILY

My mother's mother a twin,
all my second cousins
are having twins
their second pregnancy.
Our bodies spiral,
the double helix,
a ricochet of nerves and sinew.

What if my father's father's
electrocution at the
Kennecott Copper Mines,
and my father's mother's
death—her nightgown
on fire, rolling herself
in the living room rug—
still burn inside me?

What if my mother's cancer
crawls under my skin,
plumping my cells;
what if it's packed
in the meat locker of the body?

I force myself to run
faster, swim harder,
outdistance everything,
to leave my body behind
while I urge it along.

STEPTOE BUTTE

The man we asked for directions
had a hand the shape of a peony,
one blossom in dry country.

We're travelling light—
that stubble, this river,
too many bandages in common.

From this height
my field glasses contain
blank and white

acres of ruined wheat.
It's someone else's land
sculpted around moraines,

quilted with soil. Clouds
form an aperture above us—
a cloudless lens.

There's too much and too little.
We call the wind a fossil,
try photographing all of it.

NAUVOO, ILLINOIS

I visit the dead town, the restored town,
on a blind Sunday: the shuttles working,
the town weaving again, the windows
covered with translucent hides.

When the Mormons were burned out,
they threw their pottery down the wells.
Now someone puts it back together,
shard by shard.

The herb garden is tamped down
and covered with evergreen branches.
Blood stains the floor of a tack room,
but the livery is spotless, the harnesses supple.

A rifle was invented here
in the old gunnery—see one knot
in the stock under glass—
Browning automatic, long range.

I hear my own voice calling down the well
for lost ancestors: the limestone cutter,
the spinner, the tallow dipper.
I'm looking for my occupation and my name.

SWIMMING LESSONS FOR THE DEAD

*Else what shall they do which are
baptized for the dead, if the dead
rise not at all?*
1 Corinthians 15:29

I was baptized by immersion when I was eight.
At fast-and-testimony meeting, the elders
laid their hands on my head to give me
the gift of the Holy Ghost. I could feel
their hands, like ballast, for days.

At twelve, I was baptized for the dead
in an underground font supported by twelve gold oxen.
After each female ancestor's name was called out,
I was pressed underwater in my white dress.
I saw a clothesline full of white garments, hands.

Now, I dream of a swimming pool full of the dead—
my particular dead. Their bodies float
on the surface like small white liferafts;
their waterwings whisper and rustle
as they drift and spin against each other.

Flutter and fin, I tell them.
If one starts to sink, I dive in
and come up under the shoulders:
breathe out, breathe in.
I am the lifeguard and the deathguard.

IV

WITNESS

You are on the witness stand
telling everything you remember
when suddenly you're not sure
if you *are* the woman
to whom this story happened.

You are not sure you can go on
talking. You know it happened,
but to whom? You have had to deny
too much: The breaking glass.

A scream. His knife.
The blacking-out.
The forced walk up the canyon.
The barbed wire.

You have memorized the sheets
of prepared testimony—
what you have said before,
under oath to the Grand Jury.
You lose sensation in your left foot.

You feel you are inside
an old-fashioned diving suit.
When you try to speak,
vowels form, but not consonants.

You fumble undoing the staples
fastening the bags of evidence.
You have to hold up your torn
nightgown in front of the jury.

There is nothing left to trace
the path of the pain that entered
and left your body.
Someone else is telling this story.

NEW MEXICAN RELICS

Out toward Truchas,
on one of the ridges dividing the world,
a woman found the face of Jesus
on a tortilla she was making for breakfast.
And when the light is right, the painting
at Ranchos de Taos reveals a cross
superimposed on the body of Christ.

And here are the stark white crosses
inside the boundaries of the adobe church,
destroyed in a massacre, at Taos pueblo.
Low wooden fences circle the newer cemeteries,
the Spanish burial grounds. A few junipers
mark the entrances near the cow baffles,
enclosing the waterstained pictures
of the dead and the bright confetti
of plastic windmills and flowers.

Past the cemetery at Abiquiu,
opposite triangular blue mountains,
a morada stands, windowless and forbidding.
In the milder red weathered hills,
deer carcasses hang in trees,
cleanly flayed. In cold winters,
some deer freeze on their knees
before the bullets reach them.

I want to believe that a stone thrown
into the Rio Grande gorge will ensure my safety
in the Sangre de Cristos, but suspended
over the blurred grays and greens of the mesa:
a penitente death figure in its wooden cart,
a skeleton with glittering red eyes and a hatchet
held to the spot where its breasts would be.

And this is the canyon where I was raped,
where hands bruised my body the color
of sage and juniper. If I had not escaped,
would this place be marked simply,
the way hunters drawn on buffalo hide maps
are changed to dark rectangular slabs
when they don't return: mere tracings on the map
alongside how many animals killed,
and where the water, where the sheep;

Or would a petroglyph be scratched in the rock
near the grave, or a Mimbres vessel placed there,
a small opening broken in the clay,
room for the spirit to escape
to a house where a woman gave me coffee
and canned milk and a warm tortilla,
then called the police.
Down in the valley below,
people were just beginning to wake
and light their fires of piñon.

When I cross barbed wire fences,
I think of the scars on which my life is strung
and the vial of Chimayo sand
from the healing well in the sanctuary,
scented with deep earth, red mesa,
which seems to be diminishing,
travelling back from where it came,
near the niche holding a santo:
the niño who wore out his shoes each night
crossing the desert, back and forth.

RETURNING THE EVIDENCE

When the authorities
return my possessions,
it is not enough.
My camera is still coated
with fingerprint dust.
There are numbers scratched
inside my shoes,
my flute case is marked
with indelible ink.
I play a slow
and coded scale.

Everything he touched
has been given back to me,
except my clothes,
kept for "further evidence."
Violence is also evidence,
a grid laid over the body
like the red lines
that mortgage a city,
or the dotted lines
drawn on the chests
of tubercular patients.

I fight new descriptions
of myself: a victim,
a newspaper headline.
Safety was only luck, before:
a strong woman, not strong enough.
On a calm night in early fall,
I came home after the Aspen Dance:
the old men of the pueblo shaking
the branches, crossing the stream
from Blue Lake, chanting
in the clear piñon-scented air.

It could have happened anywhere,
but it happened here, where the vigas
cast strong shadows on the walls,
and the funeral home is an enormous
bulwark of pink adobe.
I want to destroy the photographs
blurred by the whorl of his fingers,
to erase the marks he left on my body.
I want to return the evidence
and forget the bitterness of touch.

A WOMAN DISAPPEARS INSIDE HER OWN LIFE

There comes a time when she has to say goodbye
to the cat, and stop watering the plants.

She wants to be more than a curator
of dissolving objects.

The song her tongue keeps
reaching for stays out of tune.

The nautilus adds one chamber each moon,
while she fills a room with rue.

She leaves a clue
inside the telephone book:

underlines the names of friends
who have already left town.

She puts on all her necklaces—
the clay beads from Peru,

the feathers from New Mexico,
the ostrich eggshells from Africa.

She wears her lapis lazuli earrings
and her aquamarine ring,

the lightning bracelet
and the tortoise shell combs.

She tries to fix one emotion
like a photograph of the room.

Someone has stolen her maps,
except one drawn in mauve

on thin parchment.
She will go there.

GETTING OFF THE TRAIN

for Mekeel McBride

Some days when the body breaks
its own line of scrimmage,
I want to believe it knows
something beyond the visible.
The signs say to get off
only at specified stops,

but I pull the emergency brake
and leap into the prairie grass.
The world fractures on a handful
of low notes. An oboe cleaves
the mineral hearts—obsidian splits
into scales as fine as mica.

I can't unleash my fears,
a nomad crossing out the simple tracks.
Like a blind mapmaker, I'm fine
with mountains and valleys,
but I can't get plateaus
or plains in scale.

Water scars on the surface of wells;
the history of oxygen slows down.
By the tracks, I find two fluted
stone fragments, ten thousand years old.
The train has gone on,
into some other future.

WHAT CAN BE CHANGED

I take a fist of yeast;
the grain of my skin darkens.

By accident, I bake a magpie
feather in the bread.

When the loaf breaks
open in my hands,

the feather is gone,
leaving a fossil imprint behind.

I experiment to see
what can be changed—

knead in stones
and the bread rises higher,

knead in wind chimes
and find a loaf of ice.

Knead pain
into the final loaf

and bake a bread
that can never be eaten alone.

V

BIRCHES

Birch bark scrolls
lie on the forest floor
in undulants of fern.

Some fragments of bark
look like player piano rolls—
birdsong hidden in the slashes.

Play on, fiddleheads.
Roll on, birch bark,
through color changes

of lemon, lilac, and peach
that striate the underside
of the bark like a palette

mixed on someone's transparent skin,
or light through old barnwood
mixed with rain.

The white, leafless birches
are like lightning flashes
among the darker trees.

Everywhere we are dreaming
that we love each other.
And always it is only
the negative rain
and the positive clouds.

LULLABY

When you don't sleep,
I don't sleep.

We lie here on a plain
of desire for no desire,

trying to smooth our gray
fissures into sheets.

Our shadows touch
when we're not touching.

We listen to the ash shift
of old fires,

the train chords far away
by the river,

the palimpsests
of peeling wallpaper,

invisible water
muttering in the pipes,

until the hissing
of the pilot light

finally carries us
into morning.

AUBADE: PORTRAIT WITH SHADOWS

Naked on the striped sheets, he lies,
beginning to wake, in the narrow bed.
The mirror catches paler bars of red,
holds light in bands from window blinds,
light which also binds his thighs.
The ceiling fan ruffles his thick dark hair;
a fugue for train and crickets stirs the air.
Now, his voice like a dulcimer might rise
to hold me in this summer haze.
Don't move, don't move, don't move yet:
I must get the shadows right, the scent
of hay, old wood, these last days
of heat, stars in a kudzu net,
to keep you here, fragment by fragment.

MOSTLY DEPARTURES

I can almost see the prairie where you are—
the flowering grasses and the cones
of white blossoms on the horse chestnut trees.
The horizon calms you after months of cities.
I imagine your eyes seek that line
as if you had cast it out over water.

A few nights ago, I saw one of the moons
of Jupiter, and thought of the night you left:
blurred lights, rain on the runway.
I can see that far moon and the slick lake
of asphalt, but cannot see your face
or hear your voice.

Our bodies lose warmth over distance,
like small moons and planets.
The words that keep coming back to me
are the ones from your deepest sleep,
from the nightmares of water rising
to cover the farm of your childhood.
I don't want to let you sleep alone,
calling and calling, with no one to wake you.

LETTER TO SAINT JEROME

Did you think if you did not love
you would not grow old?
I know you will not read this,
because you no longer read letters,
though you long for them.
You know too well the long ''o'' of longing.
Before you entered the desert,
I knew you. I knew you
before your mind started playing
patience with itself,
before your elegant fingers
traced only the spines of books
in your industrious cell,
before you reduced life to the view
from your honeycomb windows.
Now your life is pale and flowers only
with rue and the bitter herbs
you saved from your old garden.
You tried to cut the lover's knot
but not before I was caught in it.
You told me the eyes of angels
are rarely sad. Your homilies
have become more cryptic and twisted.
The traveller's joy in the garden
has all gone to old man's beard.

THE COMING OF THE ICE AGE

Everything quietly sealed over
until the world was contained
under glass like a display
in the Museum of Natural History.

Nothing was left to touch,
worse than Midas—the animals
froze in their usual mating positions,
properly pigmented, an aspect

of every season in each diorama.
Nothing could change colors again.
Humus and willow locked into place,
fiddlehead ferns never uncurled.

Moss became rigid as a fright wig
though fans were decoys to capture wind.
We could only watch while it happened—
artificial pollen dusted on the stigma,

atomizers releasing scents at intervals,
each tree labeled with indelible ink—
nothing left to chance until the last cell
gives up the stain of life.

DEAD NECK

Salt flakes fleck my skin
after a circumambulation of the island.
The rough beach grass is turning gold.
I borrowed a boat to get here—
this sand spit not more than a mile long
and an eighth-mile wide—close to shore,
but with currents too swift to swim.

Among the terns and sandpipers,
skate cases—sea purses—
scatter like seedpods. The medusae
are white grapes or moonwort,
the barnacles like lichen.

Only a few days are as whole as this,
where a cove becomes the world, trading
down to smaller and smaller forms of life:
every few steps a horseshoe crab gives way
to one more shrunken, more transparent,
until the last can't be told
from the mermaid's fingernails.

VOCABULARY

Consciousness is a singular
of which the plural is unknown.
—Erwin Schrödinger

Turning from you to pick up a starfish,
I wonder if anyone has the right
to know me this well,

the way we know the particular
habits of the day—how the rabbit
will cross the lawn after supper,

which birds fly to which trees—
and the way we fit into the double
hollows of the summerhouse beds.

Though I know the names of little enough,
when I say "eel grass" or "periwinkle,"
it pleases you.

And in your lab, when you showed me
cancer cells through twin eyepieces,
naming the parts, you gave voice

to the microscopic and asked:
"Are you thinking of your mother?"
I was so startled I could hardly reply.

A year ago on the tide flats
I walked alone and could not speak
the name of anything.

And now you turn me to you,
touch my face and say:
"lips, philtrum, iris, *you.*"

HEARTPRINT

Embroidering his name in red silk thread, your
Needle wrestles with your need to cast spells.
Repetition is the charm.
You are the woman in a hundred fairy tales,
But what you remember is never enough:
Even the blisters on your fingers from weaving
Nettles into shirts for your swan brothers—the last
Never finished—
Even the nights you were Psyche
To his Cupid elude you.
Trace, when you prick your finger, his name
For magic's sake in heart's blood,
Or for the child you were who cross-stitched,
XOX, the border around a lost alphabet.

POETRY FROM ALICE JAMES BOOKS

DATE DUE	